Lizard Tales:

Lizzie Walks On the Wild Side

by Rosemary Smith

⊕ **Strategic Book Publishing**

Strategic Book Publishing
An imprint of Strategic Book Group
P.O. Box 333
Durham CT 06422
www.StrategicBookGroup.com

ISBN: 978-1-60911-082-6

Printed in the United States of America.

Illustrations art, book cover art and book layout by
kalpart team - www.kalpart.com

I would like to thank my husband, Alvin for his patience and encouragement during this and all my many projects over the years. While we sat on the porch, sipping our coffee and watching the lizards going about their daily lives, we learned a lot about them and a little about ourselves and what really matters in our own bigger world.

It was spring! Mama Lizard watched her daughter Lizzie carefully. The day was bright and mild, and it was time for the young lizards to come out of hiding and take their places in the sun. Papa Lizard was in his chosen spot, doing push-ups to let everyone know that he was the best. He was boss of this wall and no one should come into his territory.

Lizzie was the first of the youngsters to step out from the jungle of bushes where she had hatched from a small white egg in the soil beside the wall a few days ago. There were many dangers for a young lizard that barely measured two inches long, and she would have to be very careful not to end up in someone's tummy.

Lizzie tiptoed into the bright sunlight and closer to the drainpipe that ran down the corner of the house from the roof almost all the way to the ground. She made it safely and even managed to snap up a gnat for a tasty snack. Her papa was on top of the hummingbird feeder watching her, and nodding with pride. She was doing just fine out in the world.

Basking in the full sun is different from hiding in the mottled sunlight of the bushes. There were many lessons to learn. Every day, Lizzie grew more confident, and that day she felt especially grown-up. Although she lived on a very nice wall, and had plenty of juicy bugs to eat, Lizzie felt certain that the wall across the sidewalk on the side of the garage had many more bugs and got more sunlight than her own little area of the house. Now that she came out to sun every day, Mama and Papa were not nearly as protective as they had been on that first spring morning. Miss Lizzie felt it was time to make a few decisions on her own. She was going across the sidewalk to the garage wall to see for herself how many bugs there were.

She thought very carefully about the two ways to get there. One option was to go up to the roof and cross over the porch and turn right at the corner to go onto the garage roof. There were blue jays to consider, but so far that day, she had not seen a single bird. The other option was to go down to the grass, run across the sidewalk, and climb up the wall behind the tall flowers that grew beside the garage wall. Ordinarily, she would have considered this to be the safer route, but on this day, the outside cat, Miz Hunny, was sleeping by the rocking chair on the back porch. Lizzie was more afraid of the cat than a blue jay, so she chose the higher path.

Slowly, she sneaked across the wall to the drain spout where her mother was taking a snooze inside the shady curve that led to the roof. Quickly, she ran across the gutter's edge, remembering to stay in the shade. Then she rounded the curve to the garage roof. She caught a fat mosquito and gloated a bit, thinking that she had been right and that there were more bugs over here! She headed for a sunny spot at a quick pace and ran smack into a very large green Anole lizard.

She squeaked, "Yikes! I didn't see you there! Where did you come from?"

The stranger looked her up and down, and said in a very stern voice, "I live here, young lady, and you are trespassing; you belong over there on the bathroom wall."

Lizzie responded in her very shaky voice, "Yes sir, I know, but I wanted to see for myself whether you had better bugs over here."

He blinked at her from behind his glasses and said in a clear but firm voice, "We have exactly the same bugs on this wall as you have over there, but we do have more blue jays here, so you need to be careful. Your wall is out of their sight for most of the day, which is the very reason that your parents chose that smaller wall in the first place. It offers more protection for you little ones. Now, you need to go home!"

"Yes, sir," Lizzie replied softly, knowing that he was right. This older lizard had been around for many seasons, and was usually very wise in the ways of survival. Lizzie carefully backed around the curve and headed back home.

As she got halfway across the back porch, she heard the loud screech of a blue jay. She quickly ducked under the lip of the gutter's edge to hide. The big male lizard had been so intent on watching Lizzie that he had been caught out in the open and the huge bird was bearing down on him from behind. There was a flurry of wings and a loud clacking sound as the blue jay snapped up Mr. Lizard in his strong beak. Lizzie watched helplessly as the lizard wiggled and squirmed and finally managed to detach himself from the back half of his tail and dropped into the bushes below. He landed with a plop and hid under the greenery to recover from his almost-fatal encounter.

Lizzie was grateful that Anole lizards are able to break off the end of their tails to escape from an enemy. She knew that Mr. Lizard would be just fine, even though he would not be his usual handsome self until his tail grew back. She also felt guilty in knowing that she was a big part of the reason that the incident had happened at all. After peeking outside to see that Mr. Blue Jay was nowhere around, she climbed out of her hiding place and scurried back to the safety of home.

Mr. Blue Jay was perched on the top of the gazebo, nibbling on the end of Mr. Lizard's tail with a disappointed look on his face. He obviously had expected a more substantial meal, and would have to look for something else to fill his belly today.

After some thought, Lizzie realized that she was a very lucky girl. Her parents had chosen a good place to raise their little family. One day, perhaps she would be ready to leave the safety of this wall to find her own place in the sun, but for the moment, she decided that this was a very nice place to be.

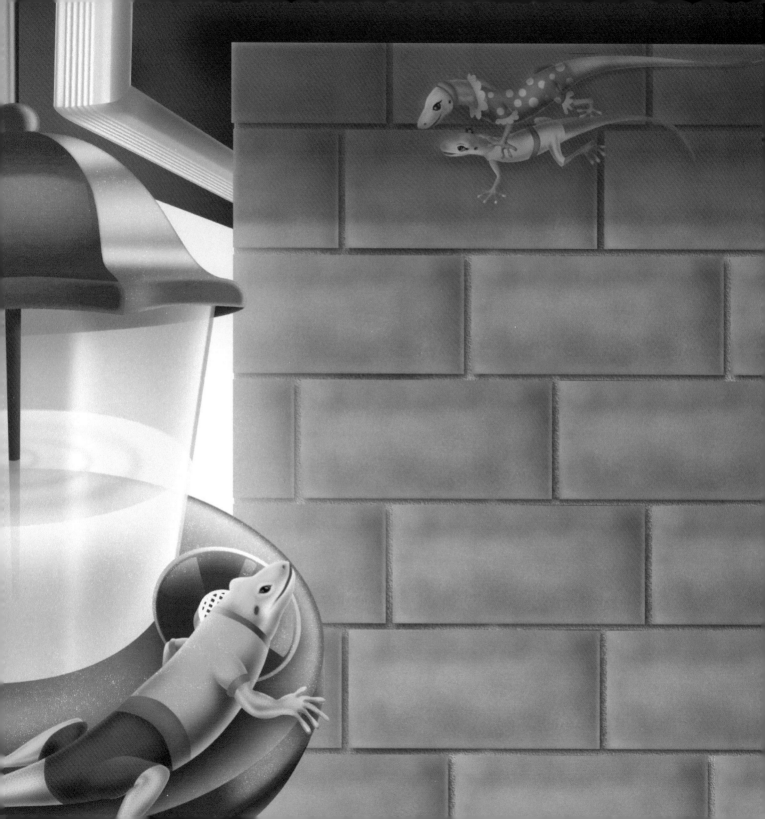

Lizzie Lizard snapped up a mosquito and smiled to herself as she slipped in beside her mother to nap in the shade of the downspout. Her father was on the hummingbird feeder doing push-ups in the sunshine. He looked at Lizzie and nodded. He had been watching the whole scary incident and was glad that she had come home. She had made the right choice and it was still a beautiful day.

LaVergne, TN USA
30 March 2011
222175LV00002B